An Artist's Night Before Christmas

By Joan C. Waites

PELICAN PUBLISHING COMPANY

GRETNA 2017

The word "Pelican" and the depiction of a pelican are
trademarks of Pelican Publishing Company, Inc., and are
registered in the U.S. Patent and Trademark Office.

ISBN: 9781455622054
E-book ISBN 9781455622061

Printed in Korea
Published by Pelican Publishing Company, Inc.
1000 Burmaster Street, Gretna, Louisiana 70053

For Gerry, for his many years of love and support

'Twas the night before Christmas, in a cute country house.
Not a creature was stirring except a French mouse.

Beneath the old stairs, through a crack in the
   wall,
lived *le petit artiste* named Henri DuPaul.

His studio glowed with a soft golden light.
He squeezed out some paints: yellow, blue,
black, and white.

The painting he worked on was for his best friend.
He brushed on some colors and started to blend.

He added more red, with a hint of some blue.

But something was off . . . no, this just wouldn't do!

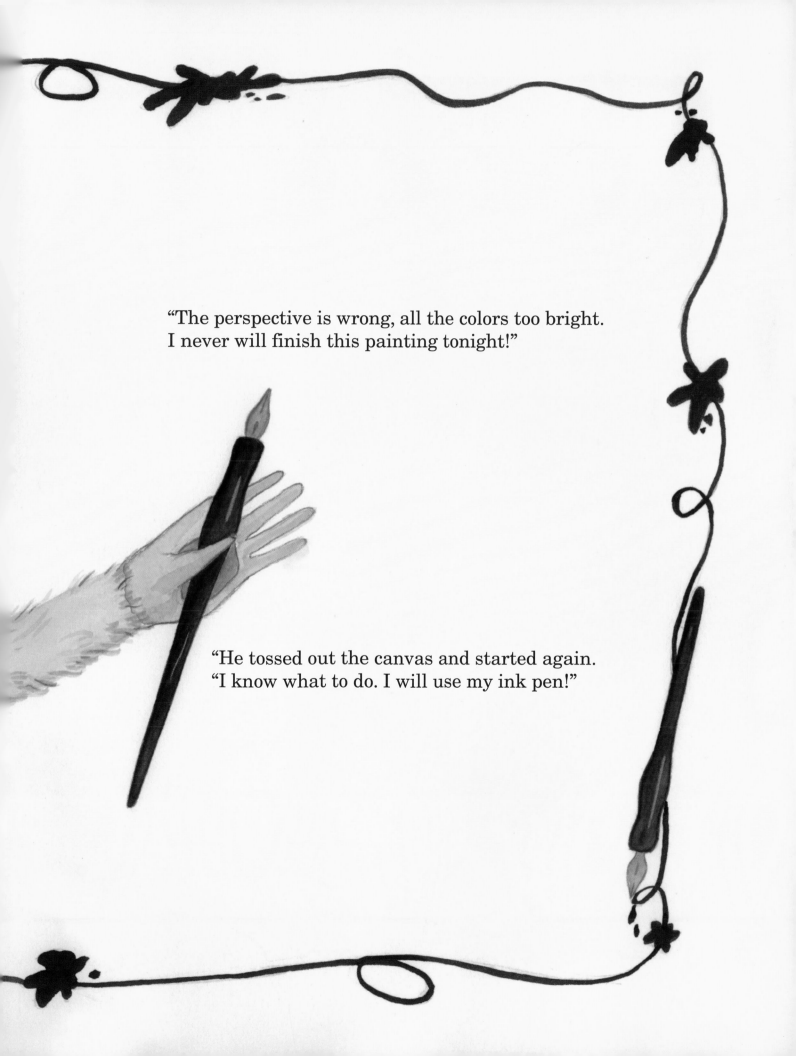

"The perspective is wrong, all the colors too bright.
I never will finish this painting tonight!"

"He tossed out the canvas and started again.
"I know what to do. I will use my ink pen!"

He stippled; he crosshatched; he varied the line.

"Alas, it's not perfect for that friend of mine!"

Just then he heard footsteps—it gave him a fright.
Oh, who would be visiting at this time of night?
Were his art friends, he wondered, playing a game?
He whispered, then louder, he called them by name:

Picasso or Degas? Monet or Kahlo?
Renoir or Matisse? Cassatt or Van Gogh?

He timidly took a step out to the hall—
black boots, a red suit, a jolly man round but tall!

"Is it you, my dear Santa?" he asked in surprise.
He blinked quickly twice and then rubbed tired eyes.

"You caught me!" said Santa. "You should be asleep.
I'm delivering presents, now, don't sneak a peek!"

"I was painting a gift, but oh, nothing went right.
I really must finish this present tonight!"

He hung his head low, dropped his brush to the
   ground.
"I wanted perfection, but none can be found.
My friends seem to paint with such skill and such
   ease.
Dear Santa, could you give advice to me, please?"

"More texture? More contrast? My brushstroke too
   thick?
I need some artistic direction, Saint Nick!"

"A landscape? A portrait? A collage? A print?
Oh, please, tell me something, just one little hint!
Some orange, some violet, some crimson . . . sky
   blue?
Or would you suggest a much different hue?"

Then Santa bent down to pick up Henri
and, lifting him up, sat him down on his knee.

"No matter which way you create your fine art,
a true friend will value a gift from the heart."

A lightbulb went off; Henri
jumped to the floor.
He'd never looked at it that
way before!
"*Merci*, my dear Santa, what you
say is true.
I will paint from my heart; that's the
best I can do!"

With a wink and a nod, Santa went on his way.
Henri had to work fast; it was soon Christmas day!

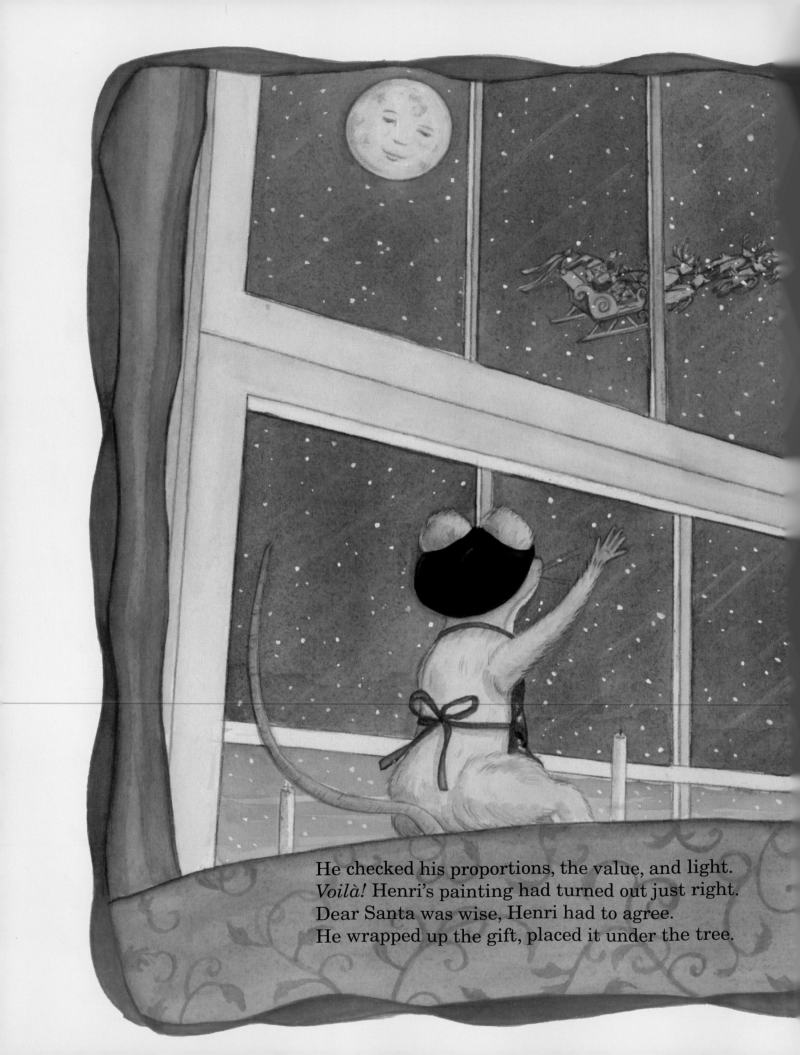

He checked his proportions, the value, and light.
Voilà! Henri's painting had turned out just right.
Dear Santa was wise, Henri had to agree.
He wrapped up the gift, placed it under the tree.

As the shiny red sleigh rose up high in the sky,
he called out to Santa and waved a goodbye.
"*Joyeux Noël!*" Henri shouted as reindeer took
  flight.
"*Merci, mon ami. Au revoir* and good night!"

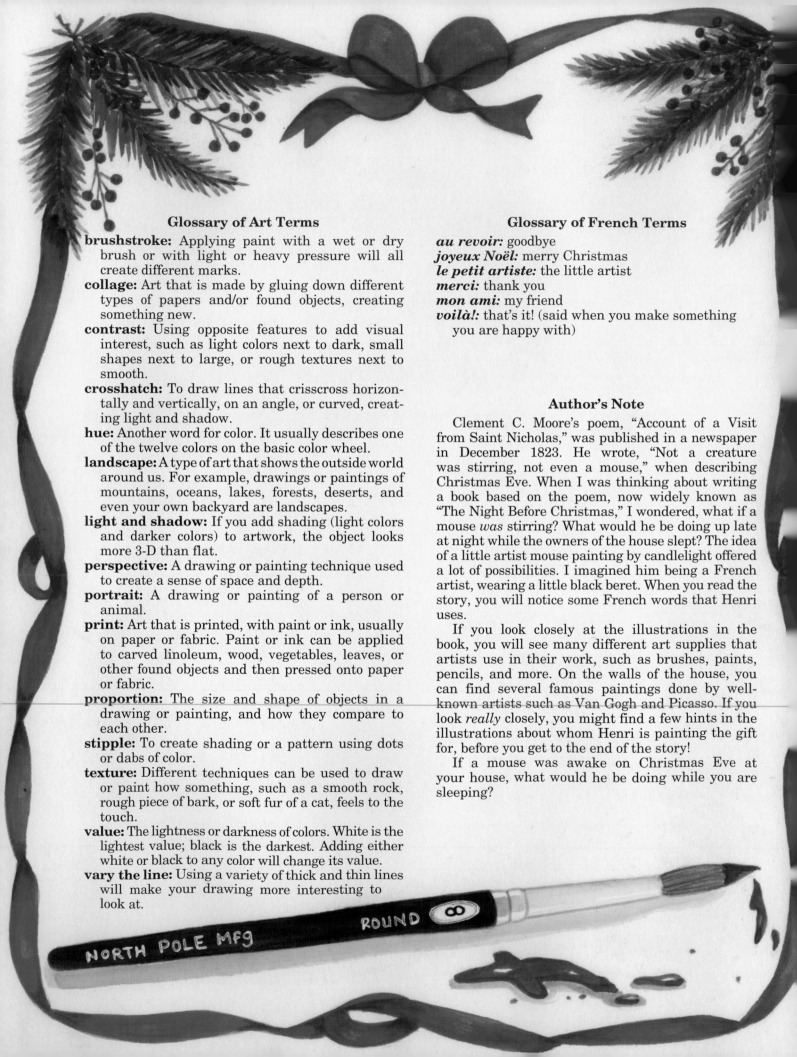

Glossary of Art Terms

brushstroke: Applying paint with a wet or dry brush or with light or heavy pressure will all create different marks.

collage: Art that is made by gluing down different types of papers and/or found objects, creating something new.

contrast: Using opposite features to add visual interest, such as light colors next to dark, small shapes next to large, or rough textures next to smooth.

crosshatch: To draw lines that crisscross horizontally and vertically, on an angle, or curved, creating light and shadow.

hue: Another word for color. It usually describes one of the twelve colors on the basic color wheel.

landscape: A type of art that shows the outside world around us. For example, drawings or paintings of mountains, oceans, lakes, forests, deserts, and even your own backyard are landscapes.

light and shadow: If you add shading (light colors and darker colors) to artwork, the object looks more 3-D than flat.

perspective: A drawing or painting technique used to create a sense of space and depth.

portrait: A drawing or painting of a person or animal.

print: Art that is printed, with paint or ink, usually on paper or fabric. Paint or ink can be applied to carved linoleum, wood, vegetables, leaves, or other found objects and then pressed onto paper or fabric.

proportion: The size and shape of objects in a drawing or painting, and how they compare to each other.

stipple: To create shading or a pattern using dots or dabs of color.

texture: Different techniques can be used to draw or paint how something, such as a smooth rock, rough piece of bark, or soft fur of a cat, feels to the touch.

value: The lightness or darkness of colors. White is the lightest value; black is the darkest. Adding either white or black to any color will change its value.

vary the line: Using a variety of thick and thin lines will make your drawing more interesting to look at.

Glossary of French Terms

au revoir: goodbye
joyeux Noël: merry Christmas
le petit artiste: the little artist
merci: thank you
mon ami: my friend
voilà!: that's it! (said when you make something you are happy with)

Author's Note

Clement C. Moore's poem, "Account of a Visit from Saint Nicholas," was published in a newspaper in December 1823. He wrote, "Not a creature was stirring, not even a mouse," when describing Christmas Eve. When I was thinking about writing a book based on the poem, now widely known as "The Night Before Christmas," I wondered, what if a mouse *was* stirring? What would he be doing up late at night while the owners of the house slept? The idea of a little artist mouse painting by candlelight offered a lot of possibilities. I imagined him being a French artist, wearing a little black beret. When you read the story, you will notice some French words that Henri uses.

If you look closely at the illustrations in the book, you will see many different art supplies that artists use in their work, such as brushes, paints, pencils, and more. On the walls of the house, you can find several famous paintings done by well-known artists such as Van Gogh and Picasso. If you look *really* closely, you might find a few hints in the illustrations about whom Henri is painting the gift for, before you get to the end of the story!

If a mouse was awake on Christmas Eve at your house, what would he be doing while you are sleeping?

ROUND 8

NORTH POLE MFg